THE HEDGEHOG'S BALLOON

NICK BUTTERWORTH

TED SMART

Percy the park keeper looked up
from his work and gazed in wonder.
"Two red ones . . . a blue one . . . there's a
yellow one . . . and another blue one . . ."

Percy was counting balloons. "I wonder where they're coming from," he said to himself. "Somebody must have had a party."

He put down his trowel and wiped his hands.

"Well, if nobody wants them," he said, "I think I'll help myself."

Percy chased after the balloons as they floated past him on the breeze.

It didn't take him long to collect as many as he could carry.

He began to walk back towards his hut, whistling happily.

Suddenly, Percy stopped. He could hear a faint sound coming from a tree stump nearby. It was not a happy sound.

"Someone's crying," said Percy. "Oh dear." He let go of his balloons and hurried over to the stump.

Sitting on the tree stump, and looking very upset, was a hedgehog. Two mice were doing their best to comfort him.

"Goodness me," said Percy. "Whatever is the matter?"

"It's all these balloons," said the hedgehog.

Then, in between sniffs and sobs, he explained to Percy how he had always loved balloons. The trouble was that he could never have them because they would always burst on his spines.

"It's just not fair!" And the hedgehog burst into tears again.

"You poor thing," said Percy.
He tried to put his arm around
the hedgehog but took it away at once.
"Ouch," he said.
Then Percy took one of his thick
gardening gloves out of his pocket and
put it on. The hedgehog nestled into
his hand.

"I think everyone should be able to play with balloons," said Percy. "And that includes hedgehogs."

He put on the other glove and gently carried the hedgehog towards an old store shed. The two mice followed.

The mice watched Percy through the window. He set the hedgehog down on a workbench and then he took a tin from a shelf. He opened the lid.

"What's Percy doing?" said one of the mice. "What's in that box?"

"I don't know," said the other mouse. "I can't see properly."

The mice didn't have to wait long to find out. Percy picked up the hedgehog and brought him outside.

"There!" said Percy. "A good idea, even if I say so myself! I think those balloons will be safe now."

The mice clapped and the hedgehog beamed. He thought how smart he must look, wearing his corks.

Percy caught hold of a bright yellow
balloon.

"Here you are," said Percy as he
handed it to the hedgehog. "Your very
first balloon."

The hedgehog took the balloon and with a great big smile on his face, he scampered off with the balloon floating beside him.

"Another satisfied customer," said Percy, feeling pleased with himself.

ercy turned to go back to his hut. But suddenly, there came a loud BANG!

"Oops!" said Percy. "One of the corks must have come off. It's a good job we've got plenty of balloons!"

"Don't worry," Percy called to the hedgehog, "I'm coming..."

NICK BUTTERWORTH was born in North London
in 1946 and grew up in a sweet shop in Essex. He now lives
in Suffolk with his wife Annette and their two children,
Ben and Amanda.

The inspiration for the Percy the Park Keeper books
came from Nick Butterworth's many walks through the
local park with the family dog, Jake. The stories have sold
over two million copies and are loved by children all
around the world. Their popularity has led to the making
of a stunning animated television series, now available on
video from HIT Entertainment plc.

Read all the stories about Percy and his animal friends. . .

then enjoy the Percy activity books.

And don't forget you can now see Percy on video too!

This edition produced for The Book People Ltd, Hall Wood Avenue,
Haydock, St Helens, WA11 9UL

First published in hardback in Great Britain by HarperCollins Publishers Ltd in 1996
First published in Picture Lions in 1999
3 5 7 9 10 8 6 4
ISBN: 0 00 762733 5

Picture Lions is an imprint of the Children's Division, part of HarperCollins Publishers Ltd

The HarperCollins website address is www.fireandwater.com

Manufactured in China